Hansel and Gretel

Retold by Carol North
Illustrated by Terri Super

A GOLDEN BOOK • NEW YORK
Western Publishing Company, Inc., Racine, Wisconsin 53404

ISBN: 0-307-10033-2/ISBN: 0-307-61033-0 (lib. bdg.)
MCMXCII

Near the edge of a deep forest there lived a poor woodcutter with his wife and two children. The boy was named Hansel and the girl Gretel. The wife was the children's stepmother, and she was very cruel to them.

One evening the woodcutter said to his wife, "What are we to do? There is not enough food to feed all of us."

"I have a plan," his wife answered. "In the morning we will take the children deep into the forest and leave them."

Hansel and Gretel overheard them talking. Gretel began to cry softly. "Don't worry, little sister," said Hansel. "I'll think of something."

Early the next morning the stepmother shouted to the children, "Get up, lazybones. We are going into the forest to cut wood. Here is a piece of bread. Don't eat it yet, because you won't get any more."

Then they all set off into the forest. Hansel lagged behind the others. He was dropping bread crumbs to help them find their way home.

When they got deep into the forest, the stepmother said to Hansel and Gretel, "Sit down and rest yourselves while we go off to gather some wood. We will be back to get you."

Hansel and Gretel soon fell asleep. When they
awoke, it was night. Gretel was frightened by the
dark. "Don't worry, little sister," said Hansel. "We
can find our way home."

But they could not find their way because the
birds had eaten the bread crumbs!

Hansel and Gretel walked all that night and all the next morning.

All of a sudden they saw before them a little house. "It's the loveliest house I've ever seen," said Gretel. "It looks good enough to eat!"

That was because the house was made of gingerbread.

They eagerly ran to it. Hansel ate a piece of the roof, and Gretel ate some of a window. Both were delicious.

Suddenly the door of the house opened, and out came an old woman leaning on a cane. She was very ugly, but she spoke very sweetly. "Come in," she said. "You two little dears must be hungry. Come in, and I'll give you some food."

She led them inside, and there on a table were
pancakes, pears, nuts, apples, and honey. "Come,
little ones," she said. "Eat as much as you like."

Then she led them to two little soft beds
and said, "Come, I'll tuck you in. You must be
very tired."

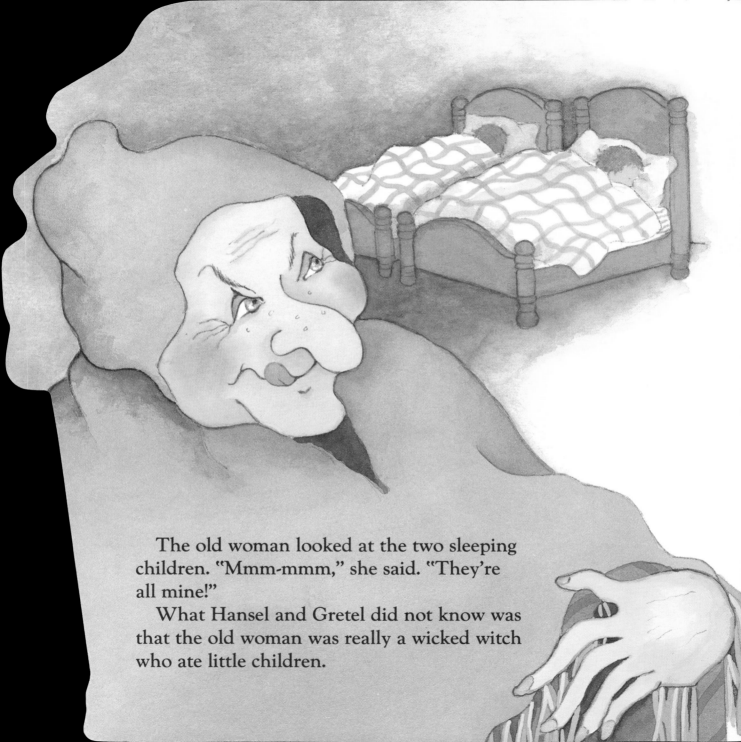

The old woman looked at the two sleeping children. "Mmm-mmm," she said. "They're all mine!"

What Hansel and Gretel did not know was that the old woman was really a wicked witch who ate little children.

The next morning the witch yanked Hansel out of bed and locked him up in a cage. Then she put Gretel to work. "In good time, I'm going to eat you both. But first you can do some of my work, little girl."

So Gretel had to cook big pots of food for Hansel to eat. The witch wanted to fatten him up. Each day she would ask Hansel to stick out his finger so she could see how fat it was. But Hansel stuck out a skinny chicken bone. Since the witch was so old, she couldn't see very well.

When Hansel didn't seem to be getting fat, the old witch cried, "I can't wait any longer. I'm going to eat you tonight!"

The witch built a fire in the stove. Then she said to Gretel, "Stick your head in the oven and see if it is hot enough."

But Gretel knew the witch was going to push her in and roast her. So she said to the witch, "I don't know how."

"Silly little girl," said the witch. "I'll show you."
She bent down and stuck her head in the oven.
With a big shove, Gretel pushed the witch inside
and slammed the door shut! And that was the end
of the witch.

"Hansel, we're free," cried Gretel. She quickly let him out of his cage. The two hugged each other and danced around the room. In every corner they saw chests filled with pearls and precious stones. They stuffed their pockets full and ran out into the forest to find their way home.

Soon they heard their father shouting, "Hansel, Gretel, I'm so glad I found you. It's all right to come home. Your stepmother has left."

With the money from the witch's treasure, Hansel and Gretel and their father were never hungry again. They lived happily ever after.